Illustrated by
Lorna Radbourne

Written by
Sally-Anne Peek

For Toots - S.A.P

For Matthew and Fiona - L.C.R

Published in association with
Bear With Us Productions

© 2022 Sally-Anne Peek
Stuck in The Mud

The right of Sally-Anne Peek as the
author of this work has been asserted
by her in accordance with the Copyright
Designs and Patents Act 1988.
All rights reserved, including the right of
reproduction in whole or part in any form.

ISBN: 978-1-7391711-1-7

www.justbearwithus.com

Icon made by Vector Market from www.flaticon.com

Illustrated by
Lorna Radbourne

Written by
Sally-Anne Peek

When the rain stopped, Eleanor put on her coat, wellies and scarf and headed out to the barn.

Between her and the barn was an enormous muddy puddle.

"I am **brave**, I am **strong**, and I **will** carry on,"

whispered Eleanor nervously, as she slipped and slithered into the puddle.

**Squish, squelch,
Squish, squelch,
Squish, squelch,**

went her wellies
through the mud,
followed by a great big

...sQuERCH!

Eleanor called for help.

"I am **brave**, I am **strong**, but I **need help** to carry on!"

Duck heard Eleanor's call.
"What's the problem?" quacked Duck.

"I'm stuck in the mud,"
explained Eleanor.
"Can you help me please?"

"**Follow me,**" said Duck determinedly, "we can waddle through the mud together to the other side."

Eleanor tried waddling like Duck,
but the mud went
**Squish, squelch,
Squish, squelch,
Squish, squelch,**

...SQUERCH!

"I am **brave**, I am **strong**,
but I need **more help** to carry on!"
yelled Eleanor.

Duck waddled to the edge of the
mud, sat down, and waited.

Along tiptoed Cat.
"What seems to be the problem?"
purred Cat.

"I'm stuck in the mud,"
muttered Eleanor.
"Can you help me please?"

"**Follow me,**" said Cat caringly, "we can creep across the mud together to the other side."

Eleanor tried creeping like Cat,
but the mud went
Squish, squelch,
Squish, squelch,
Squish, squelch,

...SQUERCH!

Eleanor shouted to Cat and Duck,
"I am **brave**, I am **strong**,
but I need **extra help** to carry on!"

Cat crept to the edge of the mud,
sat down next to Duck, and waited.

Along shuffled Badger.
"What's the problem?"
boomed Badger.

"I'm stuck in the mud,"
replied Eleanor.
"Can you help me please?"

"**Follow me,**" said Badger boldly, "we can scurry through the mud together to the other side."

Eleanor tried scurrying like Badger,
but the mud went
Squish, squelch,
Squish, squelch,
Squish, squelch,

...SQUERCH!

"I am **brave**, I am **strong**,
but I need **even more** help to carry
on," declared Eleanor.

Badger scurried to the edge of the mud,
sat down next to Cat and Duck when…

along bounced Dog.
"What's all the commotion?"
panted Dog.

"I'm stuck in the mud,"
answered Eleanor.
"Can you help me please?"

"**Follow me,**" said Dog daringly, "we can scamper over the mud together to the other side."

Eleanor tried scampering like Dog,

but the mud went

Squish, squelch,

Squish, squelch,

Squish, squelch,

...**SQUERCH!**

Dog, Badger, Cat, and Duck were planning what to do next, when Pig appeared from the corner of the barn.

"Yipppeee! Bath time!"
said Pig excitedly.

The **SPLASH** was so big,

Covered in mud, everyone cheered.

"So, who is going back for my wellies?" teased Eleanor.

They all laughed and replied,
"We are **brave**, we are **strong**,
and **together** we carry on!"

Printed in Great Britain
by Amazon